buri...
can se...

But why d... ...ne Ninth Legion ever come back? And the Eagle, that great gold and silver bird, which carried the honour of a Legion's name . . . why was it buried?

In the year AD 127, Marcus Aquila, a young Roman officer, comes to Britain. His father disappeared with the Ninth and Marcus cares deeply about the Legion's honour and the lost Eagle. It would be madness, even with a friend, for a Roman to travel among the wild Caledonians north of Hadrian's Wall, but when the chance comes, Marcus takes it . . .

OXFORD BOOKWORMS LIBRARY

Thriller & Adventure

The Eagle of the Ninth

Stage 4 (1400 headwords)

Series Editor: Jennifer Bassett
Founder Editor: Tricia Hedge
Activities Editors: Jennifer Bassett and Alison Baxter

ROSEMARY SUTCLIFF

The Eagle of the Ninth

Retold by
John Escott

OXFORD UNIVERSITY PRESS
2000

Oxford University Press
Great Clarendon Street, Oxford OX2 6DP

Oxford New York
Athens Auckland Bangkok Bogotá Buenos Aires Calcutta Cape Town
Chennai Dar es Salaam Delhi Florence Hong Kong Istanbul Karachi
Kuala Lumpur Madrid Melbourne Mexico City Mumbai Nairobi
Paris São Paulo Shanghai Singapore Taipei Tokyo Toronto Warsaw
and associated companies in
Berlin Ibadan

OXFORD and OXFORD ENGLISH
are trade marks of Oxford University Press

ISBN 0 19 423033 3

First published by Oxford University Press 1954

Second impression 2000

First published in Oxford Bookworms 1995
This second edition published in the Oxford Bookworms Library 2000

Illustrated by Ron Tiner
Map on p30 by Jonathon Heap

Typeset by Wyvern Typesetting Ltd, Bristol
Printed in Spain by Unigraf s.l.

CONTENTS

1
THE FORT

The Roman soldiers marched along the dusty road to Isca Dumnoniorum, with their Commander at the front of them. These six hundred men were part of the Second Legion of the Roman Army, and the sun shone brightly on the Legion's Eagle, held proudly above the men's heads on its staff. The road was busy with travellers – sometimes a group of tribesmen from farther west, or eye-doctors, or country people taking cows from village to village – but all moved to one side to let the soldiers pass.

The road was busy with travellers.

Isca Dumnoniorum was on the side of a hill, and the road went through the town and up to the fort at the top. As they marched, the soldiers saw the blue smoke of many cooking-fires, women sitting in doorways, and dogs looking for food in dark corners. It was still a very British town; only the strong walls of the fort were Roman. Most of Britain was now under Roman control, but it was still necessary to keep soldiers in every town. From time to time the British still tried to fight, and only a few had accepted the Roman way of life. The British lived in their little houses, and the Romans in their strong, well-built forts. The two worlds did not meet very often.

The new Roman Commander marching to Isca Dumnoniorum was Marcus Flavius Aquila. He was only nineteen, and this was his first command. For most of his life, he had lived on the family farm in Italy with his mother. His father had been a commander in the Ninth Legion, fighting the enemies of Rome in Egypt and Britain. So Marcus had not seen his father often, but he remembered a dark man who laughed a lot, who taught him to fish, and who loved army life. One day the Ninth Legion marched north to fight the tribes beyond Hadrian's Wall. Four thousand men, with their Legion's Eagle carried proudly in front of them – and not one of them had ever come back. No one knew what had happened. The disappearance of the Ninth Legion was still a complete mystery.

Marcus had asked to come to Britain, partly because his father's older brother, Uncle Aquila, lived there, but mostly because he hoped to hear news of the lost legion.

He looked up at the fort of Isca Dumnoniorum, where it stood on the hill, dark with shadows against the evening sky. 'This place will be my life for the next year,' he thought. And he marched on towards it.

At the fort, Marcus was welcomed by Quintus Hilarion, the Commander who was leaving the next day.

'I'm glad you've come,' said Hilarion. 'This town's too quiet, and I'm looking forward to my holiday.' He was standing beside the window in the Commander's room, looking out at the night sky. 'You've brought good weather, but don't expect it to go on. It always rains, here in the south-west. Or there's a mist thick enough to come between a man and his own feet!' He looked at Marcus. 'Have you any family living here in Britain?'

'I have an uncle at Calleva,' said Marcus, 'but I have not yet met him. I have no family at home in Rome.'

'Father and mother both dead?' asked Hilarion.

'Yes. My father went with the Ninth Legion.'

'You mean when they—'

'Disappeared. Yes.'

'That was bad,' said Hilarion, shaking his head. 'There were a lot of ugly stories – and there still are. And they did lose the Legion's Eagle.'

It was a terrible thing for a Roman Legion to lose its Eagle to an enemy. That great proud bird, with its silver wings, carried the honour of the Legion's name, and the honour of every fighting man in the Legion.

Marcus was quick to answer. 'It's not surprising that the Eagle did not come back, because not one *man* came back!'

'I didn't mean to question your father's honour, Marcus,' Hilarion said. 'There's no need to be angry.'

He smiled at Marcus, and after a moment Marcus smiled back.

'Have you any advice for me?' he said. 'I'm new to this country.'

'Trouble can come suddenly,' replied Hilarion. 'At the time of the new moon, perhaps, when the young men remember old wars. They're still a wild people down here – and brave.'

The next morning, Marcus watched Hilarion and his men march out of the fort, and up the long road northwards.

Now Marcus was alone with his first command.

He soon got used to life at the fort and began to know the people there. There was the doctor, who was a quiet, gentle man. And Drusillus, Marcus's second-in-command, who was an experienced soldier and a great help to Marcus that summer. The days started early and ended late. In between came the work of keeping the soldiers ready to fight, and sending some out into the forests and villages, on patrol. It was hard work, but it was work that Marcus loved.

The summer passed, and it was the middle of a moonlit September night when Marcus was woken from his sleep by a guard. 'What is it?' he asked.

'There are the sounds of something moving between the fort and the town,' said the guard.

Marcus threw on a few clothes and followed the guard to the top of the high wall which went round the fort. They looked out, and saw nothing. Marcus heard only the sound of his own heart beating. Then, from somewhere below, came another noise. He stopped breathing . . . *and something moved in the shadows on the ground.*

A moment later, Marcus was smiling. 'Somebody will be looking for their lost cows tomorrow!' he said.

Lost cows – that was all.

Something moved in the shadows in the ground.

Or was it? There had been other small signs lately. After a moment, he told the guards to wake every man in the fort. 'Do it quickly and quietly,' he said.

He went back to his room and put on the rest of his clothes, then he returned to the wall. Drusillus was waiting for him.

'Will the men laugh at me?' Marcus asked Drusillus. 'It may be just a few cows . . .'

'The men laughing at you is better than losing the fort,' replied Drusillus.

They waited. Marcus's mouth was dry, and he could hear his heart again.

The attack came suddenly and silently. Shadows moved up the hill, then those same shadows were climbing the walls. A red tongue of flame lit up one of the fort's gates, but was quickly put out. At the gates and round the walls, Marcus's soldiers prepared to fight the tribesmen. Then the silence was broken by wild screams and shouts, as men crashed together in the battle.

Marcus never knew how long it went on, but he looked up to see the first light of a grey, wet day before the tribesmen went back down the hill.

'How long can we fight them?' he asked Drusillus.

'For several days, with luck,' said Drusillus. 'More soldiers could be here in three – maybe two – days, if they see our smoke signal.'

The men had breakfast and the injured were taken care of. Marcus remembered the fifty soldiers who were out on patrol. Were they still alive, or had the tribesmen killed them? He would know before the middle of the day, when the soldiers should be back.

Two hours later, the next attack came. Tribesmen ran from behind trees and rocks, screaming wildly as they came up the hill. The Roman soldiers shot arrows down at them, killing many men, but it did not stop the others. They came with their spears and swords, jumping over the dead bodies. Smoke came from a fire at Dexter Gate.

At last the second attack ended, but only after nearly a hundred Roman soldiers were dead and many more were injured. Marcus was worried. Two days would bring more men from Durinum, if the mist lifted and the smoke signal was seen. But the mist was still not lifting.

Marcus thought about his father. Had the Ninth Legion ended this way? Had his father looked out across the hills, waiting for help to come, the way he was looking now?

'Sir!' someone shouted. 'The patrol are coming back! Towards the Sinister Gate! And the tribesmen are getting ready to attack again!'

Marcus ran down the steps to the gate. 'I'm taking fifty men out to meet the patrol,' he told Drusillus. 'They'll never get back into the fort without help.'

Soon Marcus and his men were surrounded by hundreds of tribesmen. They pushed in from every side, their short swords crashing against the soldiers' weapons.

Suddenly, Marcus heard the sound of wheels and horses. He looked up to see chariots coming towards them! Each

Marcus looked up to see chariots coming towards them.

chariot carried a driver and a spearman – and each wheel carried a long, sharp knife. Nearer and nearer the chariots thundered, and there was no time for the foot-soldiers to get out of their way. Marcus threw down his sword, ready to jump at the driver in the leading chariot. It was their only chance. If he could bring down the driver, the chariot would crash, and that would stop the rest coming through. Then his men might escape, but for himself it was death.

Marcus looked up to see the first driver, and at the last second – he jumped. The spearman's weapon missed him, and Marcus crashed against the driver. The two went down together, and the horses were immediately pulled sideways, so that the chariot began to turn over.

Marcus heard the scream of a horse, then the sky and the ground changed places. He was thrown under the feet of the wild horses and the chariot's wheels. Pain exploded in his right leg, then darkness closed over him.

2
LIFE AT UNCLE AQUILA'S

On the other side of the darkness was pain, and for a long time that was all Marcus knew. Then one day he opened his eyes and found he was lying on the bed in his room at the fort. The pain was still there, reaching up and down his right leg, and he remembered what had happened. It all seemed so long ago. However, the voices around him were

Roman voices, which meant that the fort was still safe in Roman hands.

Aulus, the fort doctor, came to see him.

'How long have I been here?' Marcus asked him.

'Six days,' said the doctor.

'Help came, then?' said Marcus.

'Yes, yes. Soldiers from Durinum.'

'I must see their Commander,' said Marcus. 'And Drusillus.'

'Perhaps later, if you lie still—'

'Not later, now! It is an order. I am still in command . . .' Marcus tried to sit up, but his words died on his lips as the pain suddenly went through him. Quickly, the doctor gave him something to drink. It was milk, but with something added to make Marcus sleep.

Drusillus came the next day and gave his report. 'We thought you were dead when we pulled you from under the fallen chariot,' he told Marcus.

'Who brought me in?' asked Marcus.

'That's difficult to say, sir,' replied Drusillus. 'Most of us helped. But what you did broke the speed and success of their attack.'

Later, the Commander of the Durinum soldiers came. He was a good soldier, but a cold, hard-faced man. 'Now that things are under control,' he told Marcus, 'I shall leave two hundred foot-soldiers here, then take the rest of my men and continue our march northwards. Commander Herpinius will take command of the fort for the moment.'

Marcus had to accept this. He knew someone had to take his place until he was able to take command again. More than a month passed, and the worst and deepest of Marcus's wounds got better. And that was when they told him his soldiering days with the Legion were over. If he was patient, Aulus said, his leg would carry him well enough, one day. But not for a long time.

It was the one thing that Marcus had been most afraid to hear, because it meant losing almost everything he cared about. Life with the Legion was the only kind of life he had ever thought of, and now it was over.

At the end of October, he went to live at Uncle Aquila's house on the edge of the Roman city of Calleva. The old man was writing a book and Marcus was left to himself most days. Stephanos, Uncle Aquila's old Greek slave, took care of him.

That autumn, almost always in pain from his leg, Marcus felt ill for the first time in his life, and he had to face the end of everything he knew and cared about. He was lonely, too, as he was the only young person in the house. He thought about his home in Italy, its sun-warmed grass and its summer smells and sounds. Here in Britain, the wind blew and the skies were heavy with rain. Wet leaves fell against the windows as he sat looking out.

The days grew shorter and the nights longer. One day, late in December, Marcus and his uncle went to the Saturnalia Games in the city. They arrived early, but already the seats around the arena were filling up with excited tribesmen, and women with children. Marcus and his uncle sat down, and a British family arrived and sat down near them. The woman had fair hair, and she wore clothes that had been fashionable in Rome two years earlier. The man was fat and had a smile that seemed fixed to his face. The girl with them was twelve or thirteen, with a narrow face and large, golden eyes. Those eyes were already filled with horror at the things she expected to see.

Uncle Aquila waved at the fat man. 'His name is Kaeso,' he explained to Marcus, 'and his wife's name is Valaria. They're our neighbours.'

'Are they?' said Marcus. 'But surely the girl cannot be their daughter?'

He got no answer to his question because the Games were about to begin. The crowd became silent and all heads turned to two doors at the far side of the arena. Suddenly, these were thrown open and two lines of gladiators marched in, each carrying the weapons he would use later. Marcus watched, and decided they were probably all slaves. They stopped in front of the seats where Marcus was sitting and he found himself looking at a man of about his own age. The young slave was short and strong-looking, but it was the look of fear in his grey eyes that Marcus noticed. Not for the first time Marcus thought that – slaves or not – fighting to the death for the amusement of the crowd was wrong.

The first fight was between wolves and a brown bear. The bear did not want to fight and, after killing two wolves, was itself killed and its body pulled away.

The first fight was between wolves and a bear.

Marcus looked at the girl with the golden eyes and saw that she was sick with horror. He was suddenly angry with Kaeso for bringing her to see a thing like this, and then angry with everyone in the crowd who was enjoying these horrors.

After a few gladiator fights, two slaves came into the arena, the first carrying a sword and a small shield, the second a spear and a net. There were stones at the corners of the net to make it heavy when it fell over the other man. Because of the net, the second man was called the Fisher. This was the real thing: a fight to the death. Then Marcus saw that the swordsman was the young slave who had looked afraid.

For what seemed a long time, the two gladiators remained still. Then the swordsman moved slowly forward. The Fisher stood with the spear in his left hand, his right hand holding the net. Just beyond the place where the net could reach, the swordsman paused – then jumped.

His attack was so quick that when the net was thrown, it passed over his head, and the Fisher had to jump sideways to avoid the sword. He ran for his life, picking up his net as he ran, and the swordsman ran behind him. When they were in front of Marcus's seat, the Fisher turned and threw his net once more. This time it dropped over the swordsman and the young slave crashed helplessly to the ground.

The crowd shouted and the Fisher stood over the fallen man, holding his spear. There was a little smile on his face as he waited for the crowd to tell him to finish the job. The young man on the ground started to lift his arm, to ask the crowd to save him – but then let it drop back to his side, a proud look on his face.

Marcus looked down at the young man, lying beneath him, and the slave looked back into Marcus's eyes. Marcus quickly lifted his hand and made the 'thumbs-up' sign to save the young slave's life. Uncle Aquila did the same. Very slowly, others in the crowd copied them. But for a while it

The Fisher stood over the fallen man, holding his spear.

seemed that most of the crowd wanted blood, and a death. Then more thumbs started to go up . . . and then more. The Fisher lowered his spear, and with a disappointed smile he stepped back. It was over.

That evening, Marcus asked his uncle, 'What will happen to that young man now?'

'The swordsman? He'll be sold,' said Uncle Aquila. 'Why? Are you thinking of buying him for yourself?'

'Would you let him stay here with me?' said Marcus.

'Yes,' said Uncle Aquila, 'although I cannot understand why you wish to keep a gladiator.'

'I need a slave,' said Marcus, although he could not explain, even to himself, why he had chosen this one.

The next day, Marcus sent Stephanos to buy the young gladiator and bring him back to the house. When they arrived, the new slave came into Marcus's room, and for a long moment the two young men looked at each other silently.

'So it is you,' the slave said at last.

'Yes,' said Marcus.

Again there was silence, then the slave said, 'Why did you save me from my death yesterday? I did not ask it.'

'Perhaps that was why,' said Marcus.

'I was afraid,' said the slave. 'I have been a warrior, but I was afraid to die in the Fisher's net.'

'I know,' said Marcus. 'But still, you didn't beg for life.'

'Why did you buy me?' asked the slave.

'Because I need a slave,' said Marcus.

'The arena is an unusual place to pick one.'

'I wanted an unusual slave,' said Marcus, smiling a little. 'Not one like Stephanos, who has been a slave all his life and is therefore nothing more.'

'I have been a slave for two years.'

'What is your name?' said Marcus.

'I'm Esca, son of Cunoval, of the tribe of Brigantes, who carry the blue war-shield.'

'And I am – I was – a Commander with the Second Legion,' replied Marcus, not knowing why he said this but knowing that he needed to say it. Roman and Briton looked at each other.

'Stephanos told me that,' Esca said. 'Also that my master had been wounded. I am sorry for that.'

'Thank you,' said Marcus.

'I thought about escaping on the way here, but I came because I thought it was you that we were coming to.' Then he took a knife from under his clothing. 'I carried this to help me escape,' he said.

Marcus did not look at the knife. 'And now?' he said.

Esca put the knife on the table at Marcus's side. 'I am the Commander's dog, to lie at the Commander's feet,' he said.

Esca made a very good slave, although he said very little about his past and Marcus did not feel able to question him. Marcus's leg was getting better, and whenever they went out, he put a hand on Esca's shoulder instead of taking a walking stick. It seemed a natural thing to do. More and more Marcus was behaving like a friend to Esca;

but Esca never forgot that he was a slave.

That winter there was a lot of trouble with wolves around Calleva. Marcus often heard them during the night. At a village a few kilometres away, a small horse was killed, and at another a baby was taken.

A wolf hunt was arranged. Marcus knew that his injured leg made it impossible for him to go, but he knew that the same wish to hunt was strong in his slave. 'It will be a good thing if you go with them,' he told Esca. 'But I have no spears to lend you.'

Esca was pleased. 'I can borrow spears,' he said.

Two days later, in the early morning, Marcus heard Esca returning from the hunt. Esca put his spears against the wall, then came to Marcus's bedside. Marcus saw that there was something under Esca's cloak.

'I've brought this for you,' said Esca.

Marcus put out a hand. 'A wolf cub!' Esca lit a lamp, and Marcus saw a very small grey cub. 'How did you get him?'

'We killed his mother, then I and two others went to look for the cubs. They killed the rest, those stupid men of the south, but I saved this one.'

The arrival of the wolf cub seemed to make things easier between master and slave, and in the days that followed, Marcus felt able to ask about Esca's family.

'My father was the chief of five hundred Brigantes spearmen,' Esca told him, 'and I drove his chariot. When I was only seventeen, we began our fight against the Legion in an attempt to win our freedom. We were beaten back

Esca lit a lamp, and Marcus saw a very small grey cub.

many times before we were defeated. Those men who were not killed were taken as slaves, and I was lying half-dead in a field when they took me.'

'And the others in your family?' Marcus asked.

'My father and two brothers died,' said Esca. 'My mother also. My father killed her before the soldiers of the Legion got through. That is what she wanted.'

Later, he told Marcus about a time ten years before when the whole country was fighting against the Romans. He told how he, as a small boy, hid himself behind a large rock and watched a Legion marching north. A Legion that had never come marching back.

'I remember how the Eagle shone in the sun as it came by on its staff,' he said. 'But the mist was coming down and the Legion marched straight into it – and it closed behind them. And they were gone.' He shook his head slowly. 'Strange stories were told about that Legion.'

'I've heard those stories, Esca,' said Marcus. 'That was my father's Legion.'

3
COTTIA

When spring came, Marcus was glad to get out into the warm sunshine after a winter indoors. One morning he was lying under the wild fruit trees in Uncle Aquila's garden, staring up into the blue sky. Cub was close beside him.

Suddenly, Marcus realized they were not alone. A girl was standing among the fruit trees, looking down at him.

'Can I see the wolf cub?' she said.

Marcus smiled and sat up. 'Yes. But be careful, he's not used to strangers.'

She came closer and held out a hand to Cub. After a moment, the animal moved forward to smell her fingers. 'What is his name?' she asked.

'Just Cub,' answered Marcus.

'Cub,' she said softly, and began to brush the warm place under the animal's chin with her finger. She was about thirteen, Marcus guessed. A British girl, tall and thin, with long wild hair, the colour of flames. He thought he had seen her before. But where? And then he remembered.

'I saw you at the Saturnalia Games,' he said.

'I remember you,' she said. 'Nissa, my nurse, says you bought that gladiator.' A cool wind blew through the trees and the girl shivered a little.

'You're cold,' said Marcus. He picked up his old army cloak which was beside him. 'Put this on.'

She put the cloak around her and looked down at it, then up at Marcus. 'It's your soldier's cloak,' she said.

He smiled. 'You're looking at Marcus Aquila, an ex-commander with the Second Legion.'

The girl was silent for a moment, then said, 'I know. Does your wound still hurt you?'

'Sometimes,' said Marcus. 'Did Nissa tell you that, too? What is your name?'

'I am from the Iceni tribe,' the girl said proudly.

'My aunt and uncle call me Camilla, but my real name is Cottia,' said the girl. 'They like everything to be very Roman, you see.'

So he was right in thinking she was not Kaeso's daughter. 'And you do not?' said Marcus.

'I am from the Iceni tribe,' she said proudly. 'And so is Aunt Valaria, although she likes to forget it. My father is dead, and that is why I live with my aunt now.'

'I'm sorry,' said Marcus. 'And your mother?'

'I expect my mother is well,' said Cottia, in a cool voice. 'After my father died, she went to live with a hunter, and there was no room in his house for me. So my mother gave me to Aunt Valaria, who has no children.'

'Poor Cottia,' said Marcus softly.

'Oh no,' she said. 'I didn't wish to live in that hunter's house, he was not *my* father. Only – only I *hate* living with my aunt, and I hate living in a town and being shut inside walls, and being called Camilla. And I hate it when they try to make me pretend to be Roman and to forget my own tribe and my own father!'

'They're not succeeding,' said Marcus, amused.

'I won't let them. I lie on my bed at night and think about my home, and remember all the things I'm not supposed to remember, and talk to myself inside my head in my own language.' She stopped and looked at him in quick surprise. 'We're talking in my language now! How long have we been doing that?'

'Since you told me your real name was Cottia.'

Cottia nodded. She seemed to forget that she was telling her story to a Roman, and Marcus did not think about this either. They spoke to each other as friends.

A voice came from beyond the trees. 'Camilla! My Lady Camilla!'

'That's Nissa. I must go.' She stood up and took off the cloak. 'Let me come again!' she said suddenly. 'You don't need to talk to me, if you don't want to.'

'My Lady! Where are you?' came Nissa's voice, closer now.

'I shall be glad if you come,' said Marcus.

'I will come tomorrow,' said Cottia.

But she did not come the next day, or the day after. And Marcus told himself there was no reason why she should. She had come to see Cub, and now she had seen him, why should she come again? He had thought she wanted to be friends, but perhaps he had made a mistake.

And then on the third day he heard her call his name, and looked up to see her among the fruit trees again.

'Marcus! Marcus, I could not get away from Nissa before,' she said. 'They say I must not come again.'

Marcus put down the spear he had been cleaning. 'Why?' he asked.

She looked quickly over her shoulder into her own garden. 'Aunt Valaria says it's not suitable for a young Roman girl to go into other people's gardens and make friends with strangers. But I'm not a Roman girl and – oh, Marcus, you must make her let me come! You *must*!'

'She *shall* let you come,' Marcus said quickly, 'but it may take time. Now, go before they catch you.'

She turned and ran away, but suddenly Marcus was happier than he had been for three days.

That evening, he told Uncle Aquila the problem.

'But what can I do?' asked Uncle Aquila.

'You could say a friendly word or two when you see the Lady Valaria,' said Marcus. 'That may help.'

'Why do you want the girl to come?'

'Oh – because she and Cub understand each other,' said Marcus.

He was never sure what exactly happened after he spoke to his uncle, but before the summer arrived there was a new friendliness between the two houses, and Cottia was allowed to come and go whenever it pleased her.

But towards the summer's end, Marcus began to have more and more trouble with his wound. One night, after feeling sick with pain all day, he could not lie still in his bed, and Uncle Aquila made a decision.

'I have an old army friend who is a doctor at Durinum,' said Uncle Aquila. 'His name is Rufrius Galarius. He shall come and look at that leg.'

* * *

Rufrius Galarius's hands were very sure and gentle as he looked closely at Marcus's leg. 'Who cleaned this wound?' he asked.

'The doctor at Isca Dumnoniorum,' Marcus told him.

'He did not finish his work,' said Galarius.

Marcus's mouth became dry. 'You – you mean there are still pieces of wood in there, and the wound must be opened again?'

The other man nodded.

'When . . .?' began Marcus, ashamed of the fear he was feeling.

'In the morning,' said Galarius. Then he talked of other things. 'Sometimes I think I'll travel again, before I get too old. But my kind of work is not easily picked up and taken around the world. An eye-doctor, now, that's easier for a man who wants to move around.' He told the story of a friend who had crossed the Western Sea and worked as an eye-doctor in the wild places of Hibernia. Marcus only half-listened, not knowing that the time would come when this story would be very important to him.

Morning came, and Rufrius Galarius returned.

'Are you ready?' he asked Marcus.

'I'm ready,' said Marcus.

Much later, he woke from the darkness that had come over him and found himself lying under warm blankets, with the doctor standing beside him. A sudden pain in Marcus's leg made him jump and he gave a small cry.

Galarius nodded. 'It hurts now, but it will be better later,' he said.

Marcus looked up at him. 'Have you finished?'

'I've finished.' Galarius pulled up the blanket, and there was blood on his hand. 'In five or six months, you will be a healthy man again.'

4
THE LOST EAGLE

South of Calleva, on a hillside at the edge of the forest, Marcus and Esca stood with Cub between them. Cub was full grown now, and it was time to allow him to return to the wild, if that was what he wanted.

'Go free, brother,' said Marcus. 'Good hunting.'

Cub went towards the forest and they watched silently until they could no longer see him, then Marcus turned and walked over to a fallen tree branch. He sat down on it and Esca came and sat beside him.

'Go free, brother,' said Marcus. 'Good hunting.'

It was spring. Eight months had passed since Rufrius Galarius had done his work, and he had done it well. Marcus would always have the scars of his wound, and he would not be able to return to the Legion, but he was strong and healthy again.

Marcus was wondering what he was going to do with his life now. The Legions were closed to him, which left farming. But to start a farm needed money, and Marcus had none. He knew he could turn to Uncle Aquila for help, but his uncle was not a rich man, and he had already done enough for Marcus.

He turned to Esca. 'We've been here long enough.'

Esca helped Marcus to his feet. 'Perhaps Cub is near. Whistle once, then we'll go home.'

Marcus gave the loud, broken whistle he had always used to call Cub, and stood listening. After some moments, he whistled again, but Cub did not appear.

'He's too far away to hear,' said Esca. 'Well, he knows the way home, and no harm will come to him.'

But perhaps Cub had chosen to be free, Marcus thought sadly, as they turned for home.

Back at Uncle Aquila's house, Marcus put on fresh clothes, knowing that an old friend of his uncle's was expected. He came into the hall and saw a tall thin man, with deep black eyes, wearing the uniform of a Legate.

'This is my old friend, Claudius Hieronimianus, Legate of the Sixth Legion,' Uncle Aquila said to Marcus. 'We were soldiers together in Judea.'

The Legate smiled at Marcus. 'I'm very pleased to meet you. I never knew Aquila had any family at all.'

The Legate was on his way to Rome on business, Marcus heard, but would return to Britain soon. His black eyes were sharp and intelligent, and he spoke with the easy confidence of a man long used to command.

Suddenly, as they stood talking, they heard a noise in the doorway behind them. Marcus turned quickly – and there was Cub! He was looking at the stranger and not moving.

'Cub!' called Marcus. And the animal ran across and jumped into Marcus's arms. 'You *have* come back!'

* * *

At dinner that evening, the two older men talked, and Marcus listened politely.

'Come and visit me at Eburacum when I return,' the Legate said to Uncle Aquila.

'Perhaps I will,' said Uncle Aquila. 'It's twenty-five years since I was last there.'

'You won't recognize it now,' said the Legate. 'Although sometimes the new building at Eburacum sits uncomfortably above the old.'

Marcus turned to him. 'What do you mean?'

'Eburacum is still . . . worried by the ghosts of the Ninth Legion,' said the Legate. 'Their names and numbers are written on the walls, and the people remember them clearly, almost with fear. And there have been times when I've half-expected to see the lost Legion come marching home through the mist.'

ROMAN
BRITAIN
N
W
E
S
CALEDONIA
·EPIDAII·
NORTH
WALL.
·DUMNONII·
TRINOMONTIUM.
(Melrose)
VALENTIA
HADRIANS
WALL.
·BRIGANTES·
HIBERNIA
EBURACUM.
(York)
·ICENI·
CALLEVA.
(Silchester)
ISCA
DUMNONIORUM.
(Exeter)
DURINUM.
(Dorchester)

'Have you any idea what happened to them, sir?' Marcus asked after a moment.

The Legate looked at him. 'Is it important to you?'

'Yes,' said Marcus. 'My father – Uncle Aquila's brother – was a commander in the Ninth Legion.'

'I never knew that,' said the Legate. 'It's possible they were attacked, that all four thousand men were killed, and there was nobody left to tell of the disaster.' He paused, then went on, 'It's also possible that they killed their Legate and joined the tribes.'

Marcus's mouth became a hard, thin line.

'But I don't think that is likely,' said the Legate. 'And a story I heard recently said that the Eagle has been seen in a tribal holy place in the north.'

'Go on,' said Uncle Aquila.

'That's all,' said the Legate. 'But you understand what it means. A Legion who put down their weapons and joined the tribes would try to hide or destroy its Eagle. But if it was *taken* in war, the tribes would think they had won the god of the Legion and would be quite likely to put it in their holy place, to make their young men strong. And if there was another war with the north, a Roman Eagle would be a dangerous weapon in their hands.'

Marcus understood. 'What are you going to do about it, sir?' he asked.

'Nothing. It's only a story, and may not be true.'

'But what if it *is* true?' said Marcus. 'If the Eagle could be found, it could save the honour of the Legion's name. And perhaps then there could be a new Ninth Legion.'

'To send men looking would mean open war,' said the Legate. 'A whole Legion could not get through, and there are only three Legions in Britain.'

'Perhaps one man could get through where a Legion could not,' said Marcus, 'and find out the truth.'

'I agree,' said the Legate, 'if we could find the right man. A man who was accepted by the northern tribes, and allowed to pass. A man who cares strongly about what happened to the Ninth Legion, and who is prepared to face the dangers involved. If there was a man like that among my men, I would send him.'

'Send me,' said Marcus. He looked at the two older men, then turned and called, 'Esca!'

A moment later, Esca appeared.

Marcus explained quickly what had been said, then added, 'You will come with me, Esca?'

Esca moved to his master's side, and his eyes were bright in the lamplight. 'I will come,' he said.

Marcus turned back to the Legate. 'Esca was born where Hadrian's Wall is now. The Eagle was my father's and I care strongly about what happened to it. Send us.'

'This is crazy!' shouted Uncle Aquila.

'No, it's not,' said Marcus. 'I have a plan.'

'Let the boy speak, Aquila,' said the Legate.

Marcus took a moment to collect his thoughts, then said, 'Sir, you say it must be a man who the tribes will accept. A travelling eye-doctor, perhaps? There are many sick eyes here in Britain, and half the travellers on the road say they are doctors. Rufrius Galarius told me about an eye-doctor who travelled across Hibernia and came back alive. We may not be able to bring back the Eagle, but perhaps we can find out if your story is true.'

There was a long pause, then Uncle Aquila said, 'But you know nothing about sick eyes, or what to do for them.'

'I'll visit Rufrius Galarius,' said Marcus. 'Yes, I know he's not an eye-doctor, but he can help me get the necessary medicines, and teach me how to use them.'

'And is your leg strong enough?' said the Legate.

'Yes, unless we are chased and I have to run,' said Marcus. 'But in a strange country we will have no chance on the run anyway.'

'You are going into enemy country,' said the Legate, 'and if you get into trouble, there will be nothing that Rome can or will do for you.'

'I understand that,' said Marcus. 'But I shall not be alone.'

The Legate bent his head. 'Go then,' he said quietly.

* * *

That night, Marcus gave Esca a piece of paper. 'This gives you your freedom,' he said. 'You are no longer a slave.'

Esca looked down at the paper. 'I am free? Free to go?'

'Yes,' said Marcus. 'Free to go, Esca.'

'Are you sending me away?'

'No!' said Marcus. 'It is for you to choose.'

Esca smiled slowly. 'Then I stay.'

Marcus put his hands on Esca's shoulders. 'It was wrong of me to ask you to come with me when you were not free to refuse. No man should ask a slave to go on so dangerous a journey. But perhaps he can ask a friend.'

Esca put his own hands over Marcus's. 'I will be glad when we start on this journey,' he said.

The next day Marcus told Cottia about his journey. She listened until he had finished, then she said, 'I understand that you must go. Because of your father.' But her face was white and unhappy.

'Cub will stay behind,' said Marcus. 'Come and see him every day and talk to him about me.' He took a heavy gold bracelet off his arm. 'The Legion gave me this for the battle at Isca. I cannot wear it where I am going. Will you keep it safe for me until I come back?'

She took it from him. 'Yes, Marcus,' she said. 'And I will listen for your whistle in the garden next autumn, when the leaves are falling.' She turned and Marcus watched her walk away without looking back.

'Will you keep this safe for me?' said Marcus.

5
THE JOURNEY NORTH

The great wall of Hadrian reached from the west to the east of the country – a hundred and thirty kilometres of forts and watch-towers, shutting out the trouble-making tribes of the north.

On a morning in early summer, Marcus and Esca were allowed through to the north side of the Wall, and into what was once Roman Valentia before the tribes drove the Romans out. Esca was dressed in the clothes of his own people again. Marcus, too, was dressed as a Briton. He had also grown a beard, and was now 'Demetrius of Alexandria', an eye-doctor, and carried papers to prove this. They rode horses that had once belonged to the Roman army, and Marcus's box of medicines was tied to Esca's horse.

All that summer they rode through Valentia, going from coast to coast and moving slowly north. They were hoping they would discover the trail of the lost Legion, but Rufrius Galarius had shown Marcus how to use the medicines, and Marcus did his best for people who asked for his help as an eye-doctor.

'We've missed the trail,' Marcus said one afternoon. 'We've come too far north. There are mountains in Caledonia, and we'll not find the Eagle there without a trail to follow. We must go south again.'

Three nights later they stopped at the old fort of Trinomontium. Thirty years ago, when Valentia was

The great wall of Hadrian reached from the west to the east of the country.

controlled by the Romans, Trinomontium had been a busy fort. Now grass covered the stones in the streets, many roofs had fallen in, and the walls stood silent and empty.

They found a place where the roof had not fallen in, and Marcus built a fire. Then they ate some food and went to sleep.

Marcus woke at the first light of morning and found Esca kneeling beside him. 'What is it?' he whispered.

'Listen,' said Esca.

Marcus listened – and heard somebody whistling a song that he knew well. It was a favourite with the Legion. Then the whistling stopped and a deep voice began to sing the words of the song. Quietly, Marcus and Esca went to the corner of the street and looked round. The singer was a man holding a small horse. When he saw Marcus and Esca, he stopped, and lifted his spear.

'Has the hunting been good, friend?' asked Marcus.

The man nodded. A dead animal rested across the back of his horse. 'But there's none for you.'

'We have our own food,' said Marcus. 'And we have a fire. You're welcome to use it.'

'What are you doing here?' asked the man.

'We slept here last night when we saw rain on the way,' said Marcus.

'You must be the eye-doctor I've heard about.'

'I am,' said Marcus.

Marcus watched him as they sat round the fire. He was about forty, tall and strong and with thick grey hair, and the usual blue-painted skin. He seemed like any other tribesman, Marcus thought. But he sang a song which was a favourite of the Legion, and he sang the *Roman* words.

'I am Demetrius of Alexandria, a travelling eye-doctor, as you seem to know,' said Marcus. 'This is Esca Mac Cunoval, of the tribe of the Brigantes.'

'I am called Guern,' said the stranger, 'and I'm a hunter. My home is a day's walk to the west.'

They became silent until Marcus, staring into the fire, began to whistle softly the tune that the man had sung earlier. Out of the corner of his eye, he saw Guern look towards him. Marcus stopped. 'Where did you learn that song, Guern?' he asked.

'When this was a Roman fort, there were many Roman

songs sung here,' replied Guern. 'I learnt it from a soldier who used to hunt with me when I was a boy.'

'Did you learn any more Roman words?' Marcus asked quickly, using his own language.

The hunter began to answer, but stopped. Then he spoke, using Roman words like somebody who is trying hard to remember them. 'I remember some words the soldiers used,' he said. Then, speaking like a Briton again, he added, 'But where did *you* learn that song?'

'I've worked in towns where there have been Roman forts,' said Marcus, 'and I have a quick ear for a song.'

Guern thought for a while, then said, 'My family do not need an eye-doctor, but if you wait until I've finished my hunting, you're welcome to come with me. Later, I'll send you on your way to another village.'

'We will be pleased to come,' said Marcus.

* * *

Guern's wife, Murna, made them welcome at the hunter's home. His two young sons watched the strangers closely and said nothing.

Next morning, Guern decided to shave. As he held his head back to shave under his chin, Marcus saw an old scar there. He had seen many like it before – the scar made by the chin-strap of a Roman helmet, after long years of wear.

Marcus said nothing until later, when Guern was riding out with them to the road which would take them to the next village. When he and Guern were a little way ahead of Esca, Marcus said, 'How did you come to be Guern the

Next morning, Guern decided to shave.

Hunter who once was a soldier with the Legions?'

Guern turned quickly to look at Marcus, then looked away. After a moment, he said, 'Who told you that?'

'No one,' said Marcus. 'I guessed from the song, but mostly from your chin-strap scar.'

Guern was silent for a long time before he said, 'I was once with the Ninth Legion. Now, go and tell it to the nearest Commander on the Wall. I'll not stop you.'

'No patrol could reach you, and you know it,' said Marcus. 'And I've another reason to keep my mouth shut.'

'What reason?' said Guern.

'I, too, was once a Roman soldier. Though my chin-strap scar is not as deep as yours,' said Marcus.

Guern stared. 'Who are you? What are you?' He looked

closely at Marcus's face. 'I – I've seen you before! I remember your face!'

'Perhaps it's my father's face you remember,' said Marcus. 'He was second-in-command in the Ninth Legion.'

Guern nodded slowly. 'Yes, I suppose your beard is why I didn't recognize you at first. But what are you doing here in Valentia? You're no eye-doctor, and you're not from Alexandria.'

'My medicines are good, and I know how to use them,' said Marcus, 'but, yes, I was in the Second Legion until two years ago when I was wounded.' He went on to tell Guern why he was in Valentia, and ended with the words, 'When I realized you were once a Roman soldier, I thought perhaps you could tell me what happened to my father's Legion, and where the Eagle is now.'

Guern was silent for many minutes. Then his face became sad as he began to tell his story. 'You never knew your father's Legion,' he said. 'The beginnings of its end were sixty years ago, when the Legion was fighting the Iceni tribe, whose queen was called Boudicca. The Legion won the war . . . and she killed herself. That was when things began to go wrong. The men believed that her death brought bad luck to the Legion. Small problems became large ones; sicknesses were blamed on bad luck instead of bad weather. When I joined them – two years before the end – the Ninth were no longer proud or brave.

'Then many of the soldiers were called to other countries to fight in other wars, and the whole of North Britain went up in flames as the tribes attacked. We won battles against the Brigantes and the Iceni, then we were ordered north to Valentia to fight the Caledonians. By then there were fewer than four thousand of us.

'It was autumn, and the mountain country was covered in mist, out of which the tribesmen attacked us again and again, then disappeared before we could make a real fight. Patrols were sent out to look for them, but none came back. By the time we reached the old fort on the North Wall, another thousand men had gone – either because they had died or because they had run away.

'The fort was in a bad condition, and we had no water. The tribesmen made one attack, and we fought them off. Then we went to the Legate and said, "Let us agree to whatever the tribesmen ask for, if they will then allow us to march back the way we came. We'll leave Valentia in their hands, as it's no more than a name." The Legate refused and called us bad names, but more than half the men would not obey his orders.'

Guern looked at Marcus. 'I wasn't one of them,' he said. 'The Legate saw that he'd made a mistake and spoke more gently to his Legion. He told us we would not be punished if we put down our weapons, but the men didn't believe him, and it ended in fighting. That was when the Legate was killed.

'The tribesmen came over the walls and many of our men went back with them. They may be living somewhere in Caledonia now, for all I know; living as I do, with a

British wife and sons to come after them. Your father called together the remaining men of the Ninth Legion, and we decided to try to get the Eagle back to Eburacum. Perhaps we thought we wouldn't be punished if we managed to do that. Anyway, that night under cover of the mist, we began marching towards Trinomontium. But the tribesmen found our trail and began to hunt us. Have you ever been hunted? The worst of our wounded fell back. Sometimes we heard them die in the mist. Then I fell back, too.' Guern touched his left leg. 'I had a wound I could put three fingers in. I could walk, but I couldn't take any more. I just hated being hunted, and it defeated me. When it got dark, I hid in some thick grass.

'Early the next morning, I came to a village and fell across the doorstep of the first house. Murna, who is now my wife, found me. When they discovered I was a Roman soldier, they did not seem to care. I wasn't the first soldier to join the tribes. Some nights later, I saw the tribesmen carrying the Eagle north again. I don't know how far the Legion got, but I know they never reached Trinomontium. I've looked there again and again but found no sign of fighting.'

'What happened to my father?' asked Marcus.

'I don't know,' answered Guern.

'Where is the Eagle now?'

'I don't know,' Guern said again. 'But tomorrow I'll give you what help I can.'

Marcus suddenly realized that it was getting dark and they would have to stop until the morning. Later, as he sat

'I saw the tribesmen carrying the Eagle north again.'

by a fire and the other two slept, he thought about his father. The Ninth Legion had been like a bad apple that had fallen to pieces. It had not been his father's fault, but it had hurt him, Marcus was sure. However, one thing remained unchanged. The Eagle must be found and brought back.

Next morning, after they had eaten, Guern showed Marcus and Esca the way to go. 'Two days' march, three at the most, will bring you to the old north line.'

'And then?' said Marcus.

'I can tell you only this. The men who carried the Eagle north were of the tribe of the Epidaii, who live among the mountains of the west coast.'

'Do you know where we can find their holy place?'

'No,' said Guern. 'The Epidaii have many holy places.'

He put a hand on Marcus's arm. 'Do not follow that trail – it leads only to death.'

'I have to,' said Marcus. 'And you, Esca?'

'I go where you go,' said Esca, busy with the horses.

'Why?' said Guern. 'Now you know the truth, you know there will never be another Ninth Legion. Why go on?'

'To bring back the Eagle,' answered Marcus.

Guern spoke quietly. 'You've said nothing about what I did.'

Marcus looked at the man beside him. 'I've never been hunted, so I cannot and will not judge you.'

'Why did you come?' said Guern, anger in his voice. 'I was happy with my woman. I'm a great man in my tribe. Often, I forget I was not born into it. Now I'll be ashamed because I let you go north on this trail alone.'

'There's no need to be ashamed,' said Marcus. 'This is a trail two can follow better than three. Go back to your tribe, Guern. Thank you for making us welcome in your home, and for answering my questions.'

Marcus got on his horse, and rode away with Esca.

6
STAYING WITH THE EPIDAII

On a soft clear evening, on a hill above the Western Sea, Marcus and Esca stopped to rest their horses. For a month now, they had travelled through the hunting grounds of the

Epidaii people but had heard no whisper of the Eagle. Marcus was very tired, and almost ready to give up the search.

'Look,' Esca said, 'we have companions on the road.'

There were five men, two carrying a dead animal, and several dogs. The men were darker and smaller than the tribes of Valentia and, Marcus suspected, more dangerous.

'The hunting has been good?' he called out to them.

'Yes,' said the Chief, who was leading the men.

'Are there any in your village who have the eye sickness? I am Demetrius of Alexandria, the eye-doctor.'

'There are several,' said the Chief. 'No eye-doctor ever came this way before. Can you help them?'

'How do I know until I see them?' said Marcus.

He went with the Chief to the village, with Esca and the other men following behind. It was on a hill above a lake, and the Chief led Marcus and Esca to his house. A young man who was the Chief's brother came to meet them.

'Was the hunting good, Dergdian?' he asked.

'Yes,' said the Chief. 'And I've brought home an eye-doctor and his spearman.'

It was very hot inside the house. A woman slave was making a meal, and an old man was sitting beside the fire. He stared at Marcus with sharp, bright eyes. Then a tall, dark girl appeared from behind a curtain.

'I heard your voice,' she said. 'Supper is ready.'

'Let it wait, Fionhula,' said the Chief. 'I've brought home an eye-doctor, so fetch the boy.'

Hope came into the woman's dark eyes, and she disappeared behind the curtain again. She came back with a little boy of about two in her arms. The light shone on his face and Marcus saw that the child's eyes were very red and almost closed.

'Is he yours?' Marcus asked the Chief.

'Yes,' replied the Chief.

'He will be blind,' said the old man by the fire. He was Tradui, the Chief's grandfather. 'I have told you he will be blind, and I'm never wrong.'

Marcus took the boy from his mother. 'I will try my own medicines,' he said.

The boy's eyes were worse than any Marcus had seen, and he decided to stay until he was sure the little boy's sight was safe.

The days went slowly. Marcus talked to the men round the fire at night, and listened patiently to old Tradui's hunting stories. But neither Marcus nor Esca heard anything about the Eagle or the tribe's holy places. Then one evening, Marcus saw the Chief carefully cleaning a heavy war-spear, and the spear had eagles' feathers around it.

The Chief saw him looking. 'It's for the Feast of New Spears. For the warrior dancing that comes after.'

'The Feast of New Spears is when your boys become men, isn't it?' said Marcus.

'Yes,' said Dergdian. 'The boys come here from all over the tribe when it's time to receive their weapons.'

'Why here?' asked Marcus.

The spear had eagles' feathers around it.

'We are the keepers of the holy place,' said Dergdian. 'We guard the Life of the Tribe.'

Marcus tried to hide his excitement. 'I have heard of the Feast, but I've never seen it.'

'You will see it three nights from now,' said Dergdian. 'At the time of the New Moon.'

Next day, boys and their fathers began to arrive from the farthest parts of the tribal lands. Then, on the second evening, the boys who were to receive their weapons went away. On the third evening, the tribe came together around the edge of the lake, and watched the golden sky in the south-west. Marcus stood with Esca and Liathan, the Chief's brother, while the crowd waited quietly.

Slowly, the sun dropped behind the hills, and then, quite

suddenly, there was the new moon. It was a signal for the men to climb up the hills, and down into the valley the other side. At the head of the valley was a small man-made hill, surrounded by tall standing stones.

'That's the Place of Life,' said Liathan.

Soon Marcus found himself standing in the shadow of one of the great stones. He stared at the hill and saw a doorway, covered with the skin of a seal. Was the lost Eagle the other side of that skin curtain?

There was a sudden flame and torches were lit, and several young warriors stepped into the empty space between the large stones. Then the seal-skin curtain was thrown back and a man stepped out. He wore only a seal-skin, the head over his own head, and he was followed by more men, all of them wearing only the skins of animals or feathers on their heads. They danced in a circle between the tall stones, then the circle broke open, leaving one man in the middle of them. He went to the doorway and began to speak quickly. Soon after, boys began to appear from the dark side of the skin curtain until fifty or more New Spears stood between the stones.

The last boy to come out was followed by a man. On the man's head were the feathers of an eagle. A shout went up from the crowd. Marcus stared at what the man was carrying. *It had once been a Roman Eagle.*

The Eagle was still fixed to the end of its staff, although it had lost its silver wings. Marcus recognized it. It was the lost Eagle of his father's Legion.

It was the lost Eagle of his father's legion.

He saw little of what followed, as his eyes were fixed on the Eagle. The boys stepped forward, one by one, and were given spears by their fathers, until at last the Eagle was carried back into the dark Place of Life behind the seal-skin curtain. Then everyone returned to the village where large fires were burning and the smell of cooking came up to meet them. For the next hour or more there was much eating and drinking. Then came the dancing.

'It is the Dance of the New Spears,' said Esca.

Tradui, the Chief's grandfather, began to explain what was happening. Marcus listened politely. Slowly, he began to get the information that he really wanted. He learned that the Place of Life was not guarded. Then the old man talked about his own last battle, when he had gone south with the tribes – more than ten years ago – and had helped to bring back the Roman Eagle.

'Did you see it tonight?' he asked Marcus.

'Yes,' said Marcus. 'Tell me more about how you took it from the Romans. I'd like to hear that story.'

It was the story he had heard from Guern, but now he heard how the Legion came to an end.

'It was my last fight,' said Tradui, 'but what a fight! We hunted them to a place north of the fort they call Trinomontium. They made themselves into a circle, their Eagle held high, and we surrounded them. They fought hard, and many of our warriors were killed. The Eagle fell once, but it was picked up by their Chief, the bravest of them all. I wish it had been I who killed him, but it was another . . .'

The old man finished telling his story, then he looked closely at Marcus's face. 'He was like you,' he said, 'that Chief of the Roman Legion. But you say you are Greek. Isn't that strange?' He took something from under his cloak. 'We left them their weapons, but I took this from the Chief and I've worn it since that day.'

It was a ring, its green stone bright in the light from the fire. Marcus took it from him and held it gently. He remembered the ring. He remembered the hand of the man who had worn it.

It was his father's ring.

7
TAKING THE EAGLE

Carefully Marcus and Esca made their plans. Marcus told the Chief that they were going south again the next day. Dergdian wanted him to stay until the spring, but Marcus told him that they wanted to be in the south before the winter came.

That last day passed quietly, and when night came, Marcus and Esca lay down to sleep as usual. They lay, still and watchful, until the whole house was asleep. Then silently they rose, left the Chief's house and went towards the holy place – the Place of Life.

When they reached it, they stood outside for a moment, listening. It was a dark, still night, and everything was silent. Marcus lifted the edge of the seal-skin curtain, and they both stepped inside. Esca took a small torch from under his cloak, and lit it. They were in a narrow hall where the walls, the roof and the floor were made from large stones. Then they walked along the hall and into a large round room. In the centre of the floor was a great white stone. There was nothing else, but the darkness seemed to breathe on them, like a waiting animal. For thousands of years this had been a holy place, and the air was thick with the ghosts of the past and their strange gods. Marcus felt fear touch his skin, like a feather.

They found the Eagle by the far wall, and as Marcus took hold of it, he realized that the last Roman hand to touch the staff had been his father's.

The staff was too big to carry secretly and Marcus quickly began the difficult job of taking off the Eagle at the top. The darkness reached out to finger them, softly, and Esca's hands shook as he held the light.

At last the Eagle was free. Marcus gently replaced the staff by the wall, and he and Esca hurried back to the entrance, brushing the dusty floor as they went so that they left no trail behind them.

Outside, the night air smelled cool and clean as they walked to the lake. Then Esca took off his clothes and dropped into the water. Marcus gave him the Eagle, and watched Esca move along the edge until he could not see him. When Esca came back, his hair wet and shining, he was not carrying the Eagle.

They found the Eagle by the far wall.

'I'll know the place when I come again,' he said.

Marcus helped him to get out of the water, then they went back to the sleeping village and their beds.

* * *

Four hours later, Marcus and Esca said goodbye to Dergdian and travelled south, along the edge of the lake, then north-east through the mountains. That evening, they found themselves on the edge of another long lake, and stayed the night at a small village near the water.

The next day, as they had expected, seven tribesmen came after Marcus and Esca and caught up with them when they were riding towards another village, on the far side of the lake. Dergdian and his brother were among the tribesmen. They had ugly looks on their faces and were carrying their spears.

'Where is the winged god?' they shouted angrily.

'The Eagle-god that we saw carried at the Feast of the New Spears?' said Marcus. 'Have you lost it?'

'You have stolen it,' said Dergdian, 'and we have come to take it back!'

'Why would I want a Roman Eagle that has lost its wings?' said Marcus, in cold surprise.

'Kill the thieves!' shouted one of the tribesmen.

There were more shouts of 'Kill! Kill!'

'If you're so sure we have the Eagle,' said Marcus, 'why not search our things?'

The shouts became angrier, and Liathan was already taking the bags from Marcus's horse. Esca's hand closed round his spear, but then he let go of it and went to stand beside Marcus. They watched as their bags and clothes were searched. The tribesmen were rough, and almost pulled a ring-brooch from Marcus's blue cloak.

'Are you happy now?' Marcus asked when they had finished. He held up his arms. 'Or do you want to search us to the skin?'

Dergdian shook his head, and the other tribesmen did not look at Marcus. Now they were ashamed.

'Come back with us,' said Dergdian. 'Let us welcome you again and put right our mistake.'

They almost pulled a ring-brooch from Marcus's cloak.

'No,' said Marcus. 'We're going south, before the winter comes. We'll remember that you welcomed us before, Esca and I.' He smiled. 'The rest we have already forgotten. Good hunting to you.'

He and Esca watched them ride away until they could no longer see them, then rode on. They saw the houses of a village as they reached the other end of the lake, and the straight blue smoke of cooking-fires rising up to the sky between the mountains. They had been here before.

'It's time I became ill with the fever,' said Esca. And he began to move from side to side, with his eyes half closed. 'My head!' he cried. 'My head is on fire!'

'Sit forward a little more and move a bit less,' Marcus advised. He began to lead Esca's horse for him.

The villagers came to meet them, pleased to see them back again. Marcus told them that his spearman was sick with the fever and must rest for two or three days. He asked for a place to stay that was away from their houses, so that they did not catch the fever too, and they gave him a cow-house that was not being used.

Much later, when everyone in the village was asleep, Esca went out into the dark night. He carried Marcus's blue cloak, with some meat inside it, under one arm.

'This bad leg of mine makes me angry,' said Marcus. 'It should be me going back, not you.'

'Even with two good legs, this is work for a hunter, not a soldier,' said Esca. 'You would never find the way.'

'Good hunting, then, Esca.'

For three nights and two days, Marcus guarded the cow-house. Twice each day, one of the women brought food and milk and put it on a flat stone outside. He wondered if he ought to make noises and pretend that it was the sick Esca, but he decided that it was better to be silent.

On the third night, Esca returned. He carried the Eagle under one arm, with the blue cloak around it.

They did not take the Eagle out of the cloak until the next evening, after they had left the village and had travelled for a full day. Esca made a fire for the night. Marcus looked at the sky and decided that a storm was on its way. Only then did he turn to the Eagle, still with the cloak round it, and take it out.

'It was good hunting, Esca,' he said, holding the heavy, golden bird in his hands.

But Esca was looking at a corner of the cloak. 'The ring-brooch! It's gone!'

Marcus turned the cloak from side to side, but the ring-brooch was not there. It had been fixed to one corner, but he remembered how it had almost been pulled away when the tribesmen searched their things.

'Perhaps it fell into the water of the lake,' he said.

'I heard it when I dropped the cloak on some stones before getting into the water,' said Esca. He tried to think back. 'When I picked up the cloak, it caught on a tree, I remember now. It will be on the ground, by that tree.'

They stared at each other. The ring-brooch was a cheap one, but it was something the tribesmen had seen Marcus wearing and would remember. And there was probably a piece of the blue cloak still on the pin.

Marcus spoke first. 'If they find it, they will know one of us has been back since they searched our things, and they'll guess the reason.'

'And when they speak with the people from the village we left this morning, they will know it was me who went back,' said Esca. 'You must go on alone, Marcus. I'll put myself in their way, and I will tell them that we argued over the Eagle. I'll say we fought for it by the lake, and that you and the Eagle fell into the water.'

Marcus put the Eagle back inside the cloak. 'And what will they do when you've told them this story?'

'They will kill me,' Esca said simply.

'I'm sorry,' said Marcus, 'I don't like that plan. Anyway, it could be days before they find the ring-brooch. Come on, the sooner we get down to Valentia, the better.'

8
THE HUNT BEGINS

The storm came soon after midnight. Marcus and Esca waited under a large rock for it to pass. By first light, they were able to go on. Early in the afternoon, they slept under a tree. When they woke up, it was dark and the rain had almost stopped, so they went on again.

They rode as hard as they could. Marcus had the Eagle tied to his back, under his cloak, to leave both his hands free. They were sure that the hunt for them had started, so they kept away from the villages, hid during the day, then rode on again at night. But on the fourth evening, when they were three days away from the Wall, both of them heard a noise which made them look back with fear.

It was the sound of dogs.

The riders were a long way away, but they and their dogs had seen Marcus and Esca.

'Ride, Marcus!' shouted Esca. 'If we stay ahead of them until dark, we have a chance of escaping!'

Marcus rode for his life. He could hear the dogs above the sound of the horses, but there was no time to look back. The land was rising under them and the light was going moment by moment.

They reached the top of a hill, and the noise of the dogs filled their ears. Marcus could feel that his horse was tiring. He took a quick look over his shoulder and saw that the riders were much nearer than before.

Esca shouted, 'Down to the river before they get to the top of the hill, and we'll still have a chance!'

Their horses crashed between the trees – down towards the dark, shining river below. Esca was already off his horse, and Marcus half-fell and was half-thrown from his own animal.

'Into the water, quickly!' Esca cried, as the two horses disappeared into the darkness without their riders.

They slid down the grass and into the ice-cold water just as the hunters appeared at the top of the hill. Esca quickly pulled Marcus under a tree branch which was over the river. They heard the dogs and horses crashing down

They slid down the grass and into the ice-cold water.

towards the water; heard the tribesmen stop and argue about what to do next. Marcus was afraid to breathe.

And then the dogs smelled the trail of the riderless horses, and started to run. 'After them!' came a shout, and soon the noise of dogs and horses died away in the distance.

'Our horses will run like the wind for a while, without us to slow them down,' said Esca. 'But they'll catch them, and when they do, they'll come back to look for us. We have to go on.' He put out a hand to Marcus. 'Come on. It's better to keep to the river for a while, and break the trail.'

It was dark now. The moon was hidden behind a cloud and the hills closed around them on each side. When the river began to take them too far to the east, they climbed out and shook the water off themselves, like two dogs, before going on again.

After an hour, they stopped and rested under some rocks. Their food had gone with the horses, and they were still at least two full marches from the Wall. Marcus put a hand on his leg, which was hurting him now.

Suddenly, they heard a sound. It was someone, or some*thing*, moving through the grass below them. They looked through the trees – and saw a man leading a cow! And the man was whistling a tune. It was a tune they had heard before, and not so long ago.

The man was Guern the Hunter.

Guern smiled. 'Demetrius of Alexandria,' he said.

'Guern, we need your help,' Marcus said quickly.

'I know,' replied Guern. 'I heard about it. You have the

Eagle, and the Epidaii are after you. The Dumnonii and my own tribe will join spears with them.'

'We need food and a false trail,' said Marcus.

'Food is easy, but you'll need more than a false trail to get you to the Wall,' said Guern. 'There's only one way left to get through.'

'Tell us how to find it.'

'Telling isn't enough. You'll die without a guide. That's why the tribesmen don't need to guard it.'

'And you know the way?' said Esca.

'Yes, and I'll take you,' said Guern.

They had to take Guern's cow with them. The animal had got lost and Guern had found it just before meeting Marcus and Esca. It was almost first light when Guern came to a place where Marcus and Esca could hide and sleep until it was dark again. He left them and went off with his cow, saying that he would be back that night.

When he did return, he brought meat for them.

'Eat it quickly,' he told them.

Before it was fully dark again, they were on their way, moving slowly at first, as Marcus's leg would not bend easily after the day's rest. However, it got better as they went on.

Some time later, they came to a place where the ground under their feet began to feel soft. Suddenly, Marcus realized why Guern had said they needed a guide. It was a bog! A bog with a hidden way across it for those who knew the secret.

'Now we must go behind one another,' said Guern.

'Follow me and do as I say, and you will get across safely. If not, you will go under.'

They had gone only a short way when a mist began to rise. It became thicker as they walked, Guern leading, Marcus behind him and Esca following. Now they could see only a metre or two in front of them, but Guern walked on. On and on. There was no sound, except their feet moving through the wet bog.

Night became day, and the mist turned a grey colour as they reached the other side of the bog and sat down under some trees.

They had gone only a short way when a mist began to rise.

'I've brought you as far as I can,' said Guern. He looked around. 'They may be in these hills too, so travel by night and sleep by day. If you don't get lost or caught, you should reach the Wall two nights from now.' He paused, then turned to Marcus. 'Before we go our separate ways, I would like to see the Eagle again.'

Marcus took the Eagle from under his cloak. 'It has lost its wings,' he said.

Guern reached out to take it, but stopped. He stared silently at the metal bird, then stepped back.

Marcus put it back under his cloak.

'So, I have seen the Eagle once more,' said Guern. 'Perhaps, after today, I will never see another Roman face, or hear my own language spoken again.' His voice became rough. 'It's time you were on your way.'

'Come with us,' Marcus said, suddenly.

Guern looked at him, and for a moment seemed to consider the idea. Then he shook his head. 'I have a wife and two sons. My life is here. I wish you well. If you get to the Wall, I'll hear of it and be glad.'

* * *

The mist slowed them down, and two mornings later they were still a long way from the Wall. Marcus's leg was hurting him badly. Now they discovered that Guern had been right. Their enemies *were* looking for them among these hills. When some of the mist cleared, they saw a man on a horse, not more than a hundred metres away.

He was not looking their way, but they fell flat on the

grass and watched him ride slowly along the top of the hill, until the mist closed over him.

That evening, the mist became thinner.

'We must find a place to hide,' said Esca.

But they were too late. The mist around them cleared suddenly and a shout came from across the valley. They had been seen!

'Into the forest!' cried Esca.

They began running, but an answering shout came from among the trees, so there was no place to escape there. Only one way was left, and that was straight up the hill to their right. But what was on the other side?

Marcus was never sure how he got up there, but there were thick gorse bushes on the hill-top and they threw themselves down into them like hunted animals, and moved quickly into the centre on their stomachs.

The riders followed soon after, crashing through the bushes and shouting to each other. Marcus and Esca did not move. Afraid to breathe, their hearts beating fast with fear, they lay as still as death while the horses moved around them. A spear was pushed through, only a few centimetres away from Marcus. And then, quite suddenly, the hunt moved on. It had missed them!

They waited until there was no more sound of the hunters, and then they stood up. The mist still moved across the valley, here and there, but Marcus saw a shape through the grey fog. It looked like an old Roman signal-tower. It was possible that the hunters had searched it

A spear was pushed through the gorse bushes, only a few centimetres away from Marcus.

already, so perhaps it would be a safe hiding place for a while. And Marcus had to rest his leg.

Esca helped him across to the tower. They went through a doorway, and then up some stone stairs until they were on the flat roof. On one side of the tower was land, on the other was the lake. Suddenly, a big black bird flew past Marcus's face and away from the tower. It screamed loudly as it went.

'That will tell anyone who is interested that we're here,' thought Marcus, but he was too tired to worry.

The last of the mist blew away. The sun shone on the tower for a moment, then was gone again. Marcus and

Esca waited quietly. They knew that someone would come soon. The noisy black bird had made sure of that.

And then they saw them. Three wild riders, coming fast towards the tower.

9
ESCAPE TO THE SOUTH

The riders dropped from their horses and ran up the stone stairs of the tower. Marcus and Esca were waiting for them. Marcus hit the first and Esca hit the second. Both tribesmen went down without a sound, and did not move again. The third made more of a fight of it until Esca threw himself on top of him.

'It's Liathan,' said Marcus. 'I'll hold him, Esca. You tie up the other two.'

Liathan opened his eyes and saw Marcus kneeling over him with his own knife against his neck. Esca was busy with the other two. He tied pieces of cloak around their hands and feet, and across their mouths.

'That was a mistake,' Marcus told Liathan. 'Why didn't you stay with the rest of the hunters?'

Liathan looked up at him. His eyes were hard with hate. 'I wanted to be the one to get back the Eagle-god,' he said. 'But others will be here soon.'

'And you'll tell them we're not here,' said Marcus.

Liathan smiled. 'Why will I do that?' He looked at the

knife in Marcus's hand. 'Not because of that, believe me.'

'No,' said Marcus, 'because when the first of your friends puts a foot on the stairs, I shall throw the Eagle into the lake, and you'll never find it again. We're still a long way from the Wall, and there will be other chances to catch us. But if we die here, you will never get the Eagle-god back.'

They heard the sound of horses and the shouts of men.

'They're coming!' Esca warned.

Marcus took the knife away, but his eyes never left the young tribesman's face. 'Choose,' he said.

He stood up, took the Eagle from the cloak, and moved to the back of the tower, holding the bird above the lake. Liathan got up on his feet, trying to decide what to do. He looked from Marcus to Esca . . . and back to Marcus again. The horses were getting closer.

Liathan went to the front wall of the tower and looked down, just as the riders arrived. 'They're not here!' he shouted down. 'They got away in the mist! Try the forest, perhaps they're hiding there.'

After some discussion, the hunters turned and rode off towards the trees. Liathan turned and looked at Marcus – and jumped. Jumped like a wild cat. But Marcus threw himself sideways, falling with the Eagle under him. Meanwhile, Esca threw himself at the young tribesman, and brought him crashing down.

'That was stupid,' Marcus told Liathan, as he stood up again. 'There are two of us and only one of you.'

They tied Liathan's hands and feet with more pieces of

cloak, then Esca went to make sure that the three horses below were safely tied up.

'Why did you steal the winged god?' asked Liathan.

'I didn't steal it,' said Marcus. 'I took it back. It was the Eagle of my father's Legion.'

'We found the ring-brooch by the lake,' said Liathan, 'and later we heard the strange story about your spearman who had the fever. Then we knew what you had done. My grandfather says you have the face of the Roman Chief, and that he was stupid not to guess you were the man's son. "Perhaps it will be you who kills him," he said to me. "Do it, if you can, but also give him his father's ring, as he is brave like his father." '

'You have the ring now?' said Marcus.

'It's on a string around my neck,' said Liathan.

Marcus put a hand under the other man's cloak, and found the ring. He cut the string and put the ring on his finger. 'When you go back,' he said, 'thank Tradui for me.'

Esca appeared at the top of the stairs. 'The horses are safe. We can go west, but we must go now.' He saw the ring on Marcus's finger.

'Yes,' said Marcus. 'Liathan has brought me my father's ring. We shall take two of your horses, Liathan, to carry us to the Wall, then we shall let them go. Now, tie his mouth, Esca.'

Minutes after that, Liathan heard them ride away.

* * *

A long while later, a guard at the North Gate of the Wall was surprised to hear someone knocking on the other side.

'Liathan has brought me my father's ring,' said Marcus.

He climbed to his look-out place to see who it was. Two wild-looking men with beards were standing the other side of the Wall.

'I want to see your Commander!' shouted one of them. The guard gave orders for the gate to be opened.

Marcus and Esca came in. They were taken through several rooms before coming in front of a desk where a man in uniform looked up. 'Yes, what—?' began the man.

Marcus saw the man's face and smiled. 'Good evening,

Drusillus,' he said. 'I'm pleased to see they have made you a full Commander.'

Drusillus stared at the bearded face. 'Commander Aquila! What brings you here?'

'It's a long story, Drusillus,' said Marcus.

And he put the Eagle on the Commander's desk.

10
HOME AT LAST

Late in October, Marcus and Esca returned to Uncle Aquila's house. They chose a good time to arrive because the Legate, Claudius Hieronimianus, was also there.

Marcus and Esca told them their story.

Uncle Aquila and the Legate listened carefully, saying nothing, and nobody moved or spoke when Marcus and Esca had finished. The rain made a sharp noise against the windows. Marcus waited, watching the Legate's deep black eyes.

'You have done well, both of you,' the Legate said at last. 'A couple of very brave madmen.'

'And – the Legion?' said Marcus.

'No,' said the Legate. 'I'm sorry.'

Now Marcus knew. There would be no new Ninth Legion. 'But what about the men who died fighting? My father . . .?'

'They died with honour. But there were the others . . .

those who ran away to the tribes, and those who killed the Legate.'

Uncle Aquila looked at the Eagle. 'So what happens to this?' he asked.

'Bury it with honour,' said the Legate. 'Bury it here, in Calleva, where Legions are always passing by. I cannot think of a better place for it to lie.'

So the Eagle of the Ninth was buried with honour in a small hiding place under Uncle Aquila's house.

'At least I know the true story of the Legion's disappearance,' said Marcus, 'and the lost Eagle is home again. It will never be used as a weapon against its own people.'

Cottia had been away when Marcus returned, and she and her family stayed away all through the winter. Marcus missed her, although he had Esca – and Cub, who had welcomed him with wild enthusiasm on his return.

And then, one spring day, Cottia and her family returned to the house next door, and she came to Uncle Aquila's garden, carrying Marcus's bracelet. Marcus stared at her. It was almost a year since their last meeting, and she looked so different. There was gold at her ears, her long, flame-coloured hair no longer blew wild in the wind, and she held her head like a queen.

'Cottia,' he said, 'you've grown up.'

'Yes,' said Cottia. 'Do you like me grown up?'

'Yes, of course,' said Marcus.

'Did you find the Eagle?' she asked.

'Yes,' said Marcus.

'I am so glad! Will there be a new Ninth Legion?'

'No, there will never be a Ninth Legion again.'

'But why . . .?' She stopped. 'No, I will not ask questions.'

He smiled. 'One day, perhaps, I'll tell you the whole story.'

One spring day, Cottia came to Uncle Aquila's garden, carrying Marcus's bracelet.

'I'll wait,' she said. Then, a note of fear in her voice, 'What will you do now? Go back to Rome?'

'I don't know, Cottia,' he said sadly. 'Perhaps I will have to. I have no work and no money here, my sweet.'

'Take me, too!' she said suddenly.

'To *Rome*?' he said, remembering how she hated anything Roman.

'Yes, yes!' she said. 'If I can be with you!'

And she put her hand in his.

* * *

Marcus did not go back to Rome. Claudius Hieronimianus arranged things differently, and much more to Marcus's liking. Because they had brought back the Eagle, Marcus was given land and money, and Esca was made a Roman, which was a great honour for a tribesman of Britain.

So Marcus became a farmer. He knew now that Britain was his home, and he and Cottia began a new life, on a hill farm, just south of Calleva.

And there was a new life for Esca, with them. Sometimes he whistled the song that he had come to know so well – the song that Guern the Hunter had whistled.

Marcus heard him one day, out in the fields. He suddenly realized that slaves did not usually whistle.

'It takes a free man to do that,' he said to Cottia.

GLOSSARY

attack to start fighting or hurting someone
blind not able to see
bog wet, soft ground that can be dangerous
chariot an open vehicle with two wheels, pulled by horses
cloak a loose coat that has no sleeves
feast a large, special meal when something important is happening
gladiator a man in Roman times who was trained to fight animals or men for other people to watch
god something or someone that people believe has power over them and nature
holy place a special place which is kept separate for a god
honour the importance and good name which have been earned by a group of people, e.g. an army
hunt to chase wild animals for food, or people in war
legate a very important officer in the Roman army
legion a part of the Roman army (between 3000 and 6000 men)
master the owner of a slave or slaves
patrol a small group of soldiers sent to find or guard something
scar a mark on the skin left after a wound has got better
seal an animal that lives near and in the sea and eats fish
signal something that sends a message to whoever sees or hears it
slave someone who is owned by another person and who receives no money for their work
trail signs or marks left by people or animals as they pass
tribe a group of people with the same language and way of living
war fighting between armies of different countries
whistle to make a sound by blowing through nearly closed lips

The Eagle of the Ninth

ACTIVITIES

ACTIVITIES

Before Reading

1 Read the back cover, and the story introduction on the first page. How much do you know now about the facts behind the story? Choose the right words to complete this passage.

In AD 117 the Ninth Legion marched to *southern / northern* Britain to make *war on / peace with* the Caledonians. These tribes *liked / hated* the Romans and were *wild / gentle, peaceful / dangerous* people. *A few / None* of the soldiers returned, so *nobody / everybody* knew how the Legion met its end.

Every legion had an Eagle, made of *metal / wood*, and if a legion lost its Eagle in battle, it was a great *honour / dishonour*. In the early 1900s an Eagle *with / without* its wings was *buried / discovered* under an old Roman *town / museum* in the south. *Everybody / Nobody* knows why it was buried there.

2 What do you think will happen in this story? Try to guess the answers to these questions.

1 Does Marcus travel north openly, as a Roman officer?
2 Does he find the lost Eagle of the Ninth Legion?
3 Do the Caledonians give him the Eagle?
4 Does he find his father alive, living with a northern tribe?
5 Does he find anyone from the Ninth Legion?
6 Did the Legion meet its end with honour, or dishonour?
7 Does Marcus return to Rome after his adventures?

ACTIVITIES

While Reading

Read Chapter 1, and then answer these questions.

Why

1 ... did the Romans keep soldiers in every town?
2 ... did Marcus ask to come to Britain?
3 ... was the Eagle so important to a Roman legion?
4 ... did a guard wake Marcus one September night?
5 ... was Marcus worried about getting help from Durinum?
6 ... did Marcus go out of the fort?
7 ... did Marcus jump at the driver of the leading chariot?

Read Chapters 2 and 3. Are these sentences true (T) or false (F)? Rewrite the false ones with the correct information.

1 Marcus had to leave the Legion because of his wounded leg, and went to live with his Uncle Aquila.
2 The girl Marcus saw at the Games enjoyed the bear fight.
3 The slave under the net was too afraid to beg for his life.
4 Esca was a warrior before he became a slave.
5 Esca brought Marcus an old wolf he had killed in the hunt.
6 Years ago, Esca had seen the Ninth Legion going north.
7 Cottia was a British girl, but liked everything Roman.
8 Marcus was annoyed that Cottia wanted to visit him.
9 Uncle Aquila made it possible for Cottia to visit Marcus.
10 A friend of Uncle Aquila's cleaned Marcus's wound.

Before you read Chapters 4 and 5 (*The lost Eagle* and *The journey north*), can you guess the answer to this question?

Who will travel north with Marcus?

1 Uncle Aquila
2 Cottia
3 Esca
4 Cub
5 A soldier from the Second Legion

Read Chapters 4 and 5, and then answer these questions.

1 Why was Marcus uncertain about his future?
2 What did the Legate think had happened to the Ninth Legion?
3 Why did Marcus plan to travel as an eye-doctor?
4 Why did Marcus give Esca his freedom?
5 What did Marcus ask Cottia to do for him?
6 Why was Marcus surprised when he heard Guern singing?
7 What had Guern been in the past, and how did Marcus know that?
8 Whose death had brought bad luck to the Ninth Legion?
9 Why didn't Guern stay with the last men of the Legion?
10 What had happened to the Legion's Eagle?

Read Chapters 6 and 7. Who said this, and to whom? Who or what were they talking about?

1 'I have told you he will be blind, and I'm never wrong.'
2 'I have heard of the Feast, but I've never seen it.'
3 'That's the Place of Life.'
4 'Tell me more about how you took it from the Romans.'
5 'I took this from the Chief and I've worn it since that day.'

6 'I'll know the place when I come again.'
7 'You have stolen it, and we have come to take it back!'
8 'It should be me going back, not you.'
9 'It will be on the ground, by that tree.'
10 'I'm sorry, I don't like that plan.'

Before you read Chapters 8 and 9, can you guess the answer to this question?

Who nearly throws the Eagle into a lake, and why?

1 Esca 2 Guern 3 Marcus 4 Dergdian 5 Tradui

Read Chapters 8 and 9, then match these halves of sentences.

1 When Marcus and Esca heard dogs behind them, . . .
2 Soon after that they had the good luck to meet Guern, . . .
3 Two days later their enemies caught up with them, . . .
4 There, they were attacked by Liathan and two others, . . .
5 Marcus took his father's ring from Liathan, . . .
6 who showed them a hidden way across a dangerous bog.
7 and then he and Esca rode away, back to Hadrian's Wall.
8 but they won the fight and tied the three men up.
9 they rode for their lives and then hid in a river.
10 and Marcus and Esca hid in an old Roman tower.

Before you finish the story, can you guess how it ends?

1 What happens to the Eagle of the Ninth?
2 What happens to Marcus, to Cottia, and to Esca?

ACTIVITIES

After Reading

1 Perhaps this is what some of the characters in the story were thinking. Which five characters are they, and what was happening in the story at that moment?

1 'Shall I do it? I have a knife, and I could easily escape from this old man. But he's told me about my new master, and I think it's that young Roman I saw at the Games. I'd like to see him – and ask him why he saved my life.'

2 'This eye-doctor won't save the boy's sight, but he can try, I suppose. It's strange – he reminds me of someone. But how can that be? I've never met any Greeks . . .'

3 'It's not fair! I only want to talk to him, and play with Cub – what's wrong with that? As soon as I can get away from Nissa, I'll go and find him, and tell him what they've said. Maybe he can think of something . . .'

4 'He's a brave young man. I wish him well, but I'm not sure he'll succeed, even with that strong young slave to help him. It's a wild country up there. Still, when I return from Rome, I'll come and see Aquila again . . .'

5 'There they go. I've helped them as much as I can, and I hope they reach the Wall safely. I don't know why I asked to see the Eagle again. Those days are long past, and best forgotten. I'm a Briton now . . .'

2 Here is Cottia, writing in her diary after Marcus has gone. Choose one suitable word for each gap.

Marcus left yesterday. Cub cried all _____ – I heard him next door. I _____ how Cub feels, because I want _____ cry too. I never thought I _____ like a Roman so much. He's _____, and kind. He gave Esca his _____, so Esca is no longer a _____, but Marcus's friend. That was a _____ thing to do. I shall keep _____ bracelet safe and look at it _____ day. I hope he finds the _____, but most of all, I want _____ to come home safely.

3 When Liathan got home, what did he tell Tradui about the hunt for Marcus? Complete their converation (use as many words as you like).

TRADUI: So, Liathan! What news? Did you find them?
LIATHAN: __________
TRADUI: By a lake? Yes, I know it. And what happened?
LIATHAN: __________
TRADUI: Into the . . .? But why would he do a thing like that?
LIATHAN: __________
TRADUI: Ah, I see. Clever. So you told the other hunters to go away. And then what? Didn't you try to fight?
LIATHAN: __________
TRADUI: So they got away. And was I right? Is he the son of that Roman Chief?
LIATHAN: __________
TRADUI: I accept his thanks. He is a brave man, like his father. And he has taken the Eagle-god back, for his father's honour. Perhaps that is right . . .

4 **Here is Claudius Heronimianus's report about the return of the Eagle. Put the parts of sentences in the right order, and join them with these linking words.**

although / and / and / because / when / where / which / who

1 _____ they arrived back in Calleva,
2 _____ we could make the young Briton, Esca, a Roman.
3 _____ is the son of a commander in that Legion.
4 I have news about an old mystery,
5 They managed to take the Eagle
6 _____ they have saved the honour of the Legion.
7 The Eagle of the Ninth Legion has been found by Marcus Flavius Aquila,
8 _____ their journey was both difficult and dangerous.
9 _____ will be interesting to everyone in Rome.
10 I think we should do something for these young men,
11 Marcus, with a young British tribesman called Esca, travelled into Caledonia,
12 Perhaps we could give Marcus money and land for a farm,
13 _____ escape with it to the south,
14 _____ they found the Eagle in a holy place of the Epidaii.
15 we buried the Eagle with honour under the house of Marcus's uncle.

5 **Look at these groups of words from the story. One word in each group does not belong. Which words are they?**

1 army, attack, battle, farm, fight, patrol, soldier, uniform
2 breathe, cry, shout, sing, scream, whisper, whistle

3 bear, cow, dog, horse, seal, weapon, wolf

4 commander, doctor, fort, guard, hunter, slave, tribesman

5 arrow, bracelet, knife, spear, sword

6 bog, cloak, coast, forest, hill, lake, mountain, valley

6 When the eagle was buried, perhaps Marcus put a letter with it, explaining its history. Use these notes to write the letter. (The map on page 30 will also help you.)

- Roman Eagle / disappeared / AD 117 / Ninth Legion / sent / northern Britain / Valentia / under Roman control
- Romans / defeated / Caledonian tribes / none / four thousand men / returned / south
- last battle near Trinomontium / Eagle / taken by Epidaii tribe / holy place / mountains / west coast
- AD 127 / Marcus / Roman soldier / Esca / British tribesman / north to Caledonia / Eagle / back to Calleva
- orders / Claudius Hieronimianus / Legate / Sixth Legion / Eagle / buried with honour / house in Calleva
- town / other legions / pass by / why / Eagle / lies here

7 Do you agree (A) or disagree (D) with these sentences? Explain why.

1 It is better to die than to live as a slave.

2 Marcus was wrong to steal from people who shared their food and house with him.

3 Marcus was right to take the Eagle, because it belonged to the Romans.

ABOUT THE AUTHOR

Rosemary Sutcliff (1920–1992) was born in Surrey, England, the daughter of a British naval officer. From the age of two she had a disease of the bones which prevented her from walking, and much of her later life was spent in a wheelchair. She did not go to school until she was nine, but she read widely and became very interested in ancient history and legends. At fourteen, she went to art school to train as a painter. Some years later, however, as her disability grew worse, she had to give up painting, and she turned to writing instead.

Her first book was *The Chronicles of Robin Hood* in 1950, and she went on to write over thirty historical novels, some of which have become classics. *The Eagle of the Ninth* (1954) was the first of many novels about the Roman occupation of Britain; another, *The Lantern Bearers* (1959), won the Carnegie Medal, a prize for the best children's book of the year. *Sun Horse, Moon Horse* (1977) is about the making of the famous White Horse on the Berkshire hills, and *Songs for a Dark Queen* (1978) tells the story of Boudicca, Queen of the Iceni.

Rosemary Sutcliff was not a historian, but said that she had 'never knowingly falsified history'. In an author's note in *The Eagle of the Ninth*, she described the finding of the wingless Roman Eagle at Silchester, and wrote: 'Different people have had different ideas as to how it came to be there, but no one knows, just as no one knows what happened to the Ninth Legion after it marched into the northern mists. It is from these two mysteries, brought together, that I have made the story of the Eagle of the Ninth.'

ABOUT BOOKWORMS

OXFORD BOOKWORMS LIBRARY

Classics • True Stories • Fantasy & Horror • Human Interest
Crime & Mystery • Thriller & Adventure

The OXFORD BOOKWORMS LIBRARY offers a wide range of original and adapted stories, both classic and modern, which take learners from elementary to advanced level through six carefully graded language stages:

Stage 1 (400 headwords)	**Stage 4** (1400 headwords)
Stage 2 (700 headwords)	**Stage 5** (1800 headwords)
Stage 3 (1000 headwords)	**Stage 6** (2500 headwords)

More than fifty titles are also available on cassette, and there are many titles at Stages 1 to 4 which are specially recommended for younger learners. In addition to the introductions and activities in each Bookworm, resource material includes photocopiable test worksheets and Teacher's Handbooks, which contain advice on running a class library and using cassettes, and the answers for the activities in the books.

Several other series are linked to the OXFORD BOOKWORMS LIBRARY. They range from highly illustrated readers for young learners, to playscripts, non-fiction readers, and unsimplified texts for advanced learners.

Oxford Bookworms Starters
Oxford Bookworms Playscripts
Oxford Bookworms Factfiles
Oxford Bookworms Collection

Details of these series and a full list of all titles in the OXFORD BOOKWORMS LIBRARY can be found in the *Oxford English* catalogues. A selection of titles from the OXFORD BOOKWORMS LIBRARY can be found on the next pages.

BOOKWORMS • THRILLER & ADVENTURE • STAGE 4

Mr Midshipman Hornblower

C. S. FORESTER

Retold by Rosemary Border

Hornblower fired. There was a small cloud of smoke, but no bang. 'This is death,' he thought. 'My pistol was the unloaded one.'

But Horatio Hornblower does not die. He survives the duel with Simpson, learns to overcome his seasickness, and goes on to risk his life many times over. It is 1793, Britain is at war with France, and life on a sailing ship of war is hard and dangerous. But the hardest battles are fought by Hornblower within himself.

BOOKWORMS • CLASSICS • STAGE 4

Lord Jim

JOSEPH CONRAD

Retold by Clare West

A hundred years ago a seaman's life was full of danger, but Jim, the first mate on board the *Patna*, is not afraid of danger. He is young, strong, confident of his bravery. He dreams of great adventures – and the chance to show the world what a hero he is.

But the sea is no place for dreamers. When the chance comes, on a calm moonlit night in the Indian Ocean, Jim fails the test, and his world falls to pieces around him. He disappears into the jungles of south-east Asia, searching for a way to prove himself, once and for all . . .

BOOKWORMS • HUMAN INTEREST • STAGE 4

Lorna Doone

R. D. BLACKMORE

Retold by David Penn

One winter's day in 1673 young John Ridd is riding home from school, across the wild lonely hills of Exmoor. He has to pass Doone valley – a dangerous place, as the Doones are famous robbers and murderers. All Exmoor lives in fear of the Doones.

At home there is sad news waiting for young John, and he learns that he has good reason to hate the Doones. But in the years to come he meets Lorna Doone, with her lovely smile and big dark eyes. And soon he is deeply, hopelessly, in love . . .

BOOKWORMS • CLASSICS • STAGE 4

A Tale of Two Cities

CHARLES DICKENS

Retold by Ralph Mowat

'The Marquis lay there, like stone, with a knife pushed into his heart. On his chest lay a piece of paper, with the words: *Drive him fast to his grave. This is from JACQUES.*'

The French Revolution brings terror and death to many people. But even in these troubled times people can still love and be kind. They can be generous and true-hearted . . . and brave.

BOOKWORMS • THRILLER & ADVENTURE • STAGE 4

The Silver Sword

IAN SERRAILLIER

Retold by John Escott

Jan opened his wooden box and took out the silver sword. 'This will bring me luck,' he said to Mr Balicki. 'And it will bring you luck because you gave it to me.'

The silver sword is only a paper knife, but it gives Jan and his friends hope. Hungry, cold, and afraid, the four children try to stay alive among the ruins of bombed cities in war-torn Europe. Soon they will begin the long and dangerous journey south, from Poland to Switzerland, where they hope to find their parents again.

BOOKWORMS • CLASSICS • STAGE 5

Great Expectations

CHARLES DICKENS

Retold by Clare West

In a gloomy, neglected house Miss Havisham sits, as she has sat year after year, in a wedding dress and veil that were once white, and are now faded and yellow with age. Her face is like a death's head; her dark eyes burn with bitterness and hate. By her side sits a proud and beautiful girl, and in front of her, trembling with fear in his thick country boots, stands young Pip.

Miss Havisham stares at Pip coldly, and murmurs to the girl at her side: 'Break his heart, Estella. Break his heart!'